D0429258

Small Tales from the Big Forest

ARMADiLLO
AND
HARe

JeReMy StRoNg
ILLUSTRATED BY ReBecca BaGLey

db
FICKLING
David Fickling Books

Scholastic Inc. / New York

First published in the United Kingdom in 2019 by
David Fickling Books,
31 Beaumont Street,
Oxford OX1 2NP.

davidficklingbooks.com

Library of Congress Cataloging-in-Publication Data available

ISBN 978-1-338-54059-8

10 9 8 7 6 5 4 3 2 1   20 21 22 23 24

Printed in the U.S.A.   23
First edition, February 2020

Book design by Stephanie Yang

For Gillie, with love and thanks

Contents

Armadillo and Hare

It was a glorious spring morning. It had rained in the night. Every leaf and blade of grass was illuminated with liquid diamonds. Armadillo grunted heavily and heaved himself out of bed. He pulled on his old cardigan. As usual he didn't notice that he'd put the buttons in the wrong buttonholes. He sat for a moment and considered his feet, briefly wiggling his toes.

"I'm still alive then," he said out loud to himself, and he let off a single chuckling snort before pushing his feet into his battered red slippers.

Armadillo padded off to the kitchen and opened the fridge door.

"Fridge light isn't working again," he muttered. "And there's no cheese." He went to the bottom of the stairs and called up to Hare. "There's no cheese in the fridge. Did you eat it?"

"I'm asleep," came the reply.

"How can you shout back at me if you're asleep?" Armadillo asked.

"Because my mouth is open," Hare answered. "And sound is coming out, but my eyes are shut and no light is getting in, so I'm asleep."

"Open your eyes then," Armadillo suggested.

"Even if I do there'll still be no cheese in

the fridge. You'll have to go to the store." Hare yawned. "Anyhow, you should lose weight. Cheese makes you fat, and your stomach is getting bigger. You should exercise, Armadillo, like me, and stop eating cheese."

Armadillo didn't reply. Instead, he went into the living room and heaved himself into the big armchair. He knew he was putting on

weight, but he didn't like to be told about it. He certainly didn't want to do any exercise, and there was no way that he was going to stop eating cheese. He wished that Hare was wrong, but he wasn't. That made things even more depressing. Hare was nearly always right.

Armadillo sighed.

Hare came downstairs. He was in his dark-blue pajamas. They had little stars on them.

Armadillo liked Hare's pajamas, but they didn't make them in anything near an armadillo shape or size.

Hare paused for a moment in front of the mirror. He carefully straightened his phenomenal ears, adjusted his glasses, and draped a long colorful scarf casually around his neck.

"I thought I might buy a new scarf soon," said Hare. He turned toward the kitchen. "You left the fridge door open," he observed.

He's right again, thought Armadillo. "Yes, I did," he declared. "I thought some cheese might jump in if I left it open."

"It hasn't," Hare told him.

Armadillo shrugged. "I didn't think it would. It was just a chance. A tiny, tiny

possibility that some cheese might come wandering along and think: Oh, *that looks like a nice fridge. I could sit inside and keep cool. This warm sun is making me melt. How kind of someone to leave the door open for me. I'll just hop inside.*" Armadillo beamed at his friend.

Hare twitched one ear. "The fridge light's gone."

"I know," Armadillo answered.

"I'll make some breakfast then," Hare said.

"Without cheese?" Armadillo questioned.

Hare stood in the kitchen doorway and looked back at Armadillo slumped in the armchair.

"You spend too much time sitting down," he told his friend. "What you need is a hobby, something to do every day, something to keep you occupied. Maybe do some exercises."

Armadillo gave a loud snort.

"I shall make us a healthy breakfast," Hare went on. "Then you and I will do some exercises. I know some very good ones."

"That will be nice," Armadillo muttered.

"You've done your buttons up wrong again," Hare told him.

Hare went to the kitchen and clattered around among the plates and bowls and cutlery. He soon reappeared with a tray full of fruit and juice—but no cheese.

While they ate, Hare explained why it was important to exercise. Armadillo thought he might buy some earplugs when he went out to get some cheese.

Hare pushed away his clean plate, got to his feet, and took off his scarf. "Right, breakfast finished, so now we will do our exercises. You stand there, Armadillo, and do what I do."

So Armadillo stood there and did what Hare did. He bent to the right and he bent to the left. He did some knee bends and rolled

his head around and around. He did ten push-ups and five-star jumps. He got a little out of breath.

"That's good," observed Hare. "Being out of breath shows how much you need to exercise."

"But I'm only out of breath because I'm exercising," panted Armadillo.

Hare ignored him. "Put your arms above your head," he said. "Like this."

Armadillo stopped and stared at his friend. "Hare, stop it," he said. "Don't be silly. I have four short legs and I certainly can't put any of them above my head. I have done quite enough exercising for today, thank you. I am going to the store and I'm going to buy some cheese. Then I'm coming back home and I shall put the cheese in the fridge, with or without a light."

"Good idea," said Hare. "And you could jog all the way to the store and back. Jogging is very good for you."

But Armadillo didn't jog there or back. He put his front paws in his lopsided cardigan pockets and he walked. Slowly.

Armadillos do not jog, but Armadillo did like walking. It helped him think, and what he was thinking was something that rather interested him, and the more Armadillo thought about it, the more he fancied it. He decided that when he got back home, he was going to do some painting. He knew exactly what he was going to paint too.

It would be a picture of a cheese sandwich.

If Hare wanted Armadillo to have a hobby, then painting cheese sandwiches would fit the bill very nicely. What's more, it might even put an end to all that "now put your arms above your head" nonsense.

Armadillo was so taken with his wonderful idea that he almost ran home.

Almost. But not quite.

The Fridge Light

It was the *ping-ping* of a bell that Armadillo and Hare noticed first. Then it was the *beep-beep* of a horn.

Hare went to the window and looked out. He removed his glasses and looked again. It made no difference.

Armadillo put down his paintbrush. He had been working flat out all morning and had already completed three cheese-sandwich masterpieces. One was a view from the left, and one was a view from the right, and the last was a view from above. All in all, the subject was well covered.

"What is all that pinging and beeping?" he demanded.

Hare shook his head. "You had better come and see this for yourself."

Armadillo went to the window and peered over Hare's shoulder.

"What on earth . . . ?" began Armadillo, but he didn't finish. He simply stared.

A strange, round, furry creature was riding a bicycle up and down the clearing outside the cabin. Whatever it was sometimes pinged a silver bell on the handlebars. Other times she parped a red horn. Not only that, but there was a little basket strapped to the handlebars too.

"What on earth . . . ?" Armadillo repeated. Even as he spoke, the furry creature did something unexpected. She stood on the seat, balancing carefully. All of a sudden she flipped over and did a handstand. Finally she did a one-pawed handstand on the seat. With her

other free paw, she did some more ping-pinging and beep-beeping. Meanwhile she waggled her back paws in the air as if they were saying "hello!"

Hare was pretty good at exercises himself. He could balance on one leg. But not upside down. And definitely not on a bicycle. Or pinging and beeping at the same time and waving "hello!" with his feet. That was pretty clever stuff, thought Hare, especially for such a round animal.

The two friends went and stood outside the front door. They both watched in considerable amazement.

The strange animal sat back on the seat. She pedaled a little faster, pulled a wheelie, and finally skidded to a halt right by the front door.

She beamed at them both.

"Hello!" she said cheerfully, showing a lot of pretty white teeth.

"Hello," echoed Hare.

"Hmm," said Armadillo. He looked this new creature up and down and wrinkled his nose. "Do tell us who you are and what you are doing," he said.

"Wombat," said Wombat, still smiling.

"Really? I have no idea what a wombat is," Armadillo said, a trifle grumpily.

"A wombat is me. That's what a wombat is. Simple."

Hare thought Wombat looked rather fun. She had shiny, fluffy brown fur and twinkly black eyes. She was energetic—a bit like himself, he thought—except she was a lot rounder and her ears were considerably smaller, which Hare liked, his being considerably larger. Hare was rather proud of his ears.

"You're riding a bicycle," Armadillo said stiffly. "Is that something wombats do?"

"Not at all. It's what this wombat does. I ride bikes and I mend fridge lights."

Armadillo relaxed a fraction. "Ah! The fridge light. That's good." A frown crept across Armadillo's hairy forehead. "But why all that business on the seat? And the pinging and the beeping?"

"Why not?" asked Wombat. She seemed surprised to have been asked such a pointless question. "It's what I do. We all have to do something."

Hare's long ears waggled in agreement.

"I play the tuba," he told Wombat. He dashed into the house.

"Oh!" Wombat sighed. "I'd love to do that."

Armadillo shuffled forward. "I make him do it outside because every time he blows into it, things pop out of the top."

"What sort of things?" asked Wombat, highly intrigued.

"Oh, flames, butterflies, cabbages, even some puppies last week—we never know what to expect. Then they just fade away and disappear.

Look, here he is. Watch out, and expect the unexpected."

Hare sat on the steps and began to play a jaunty, happy tune on his tuba. Out popped several colored balls. They bounced around a few times before slowly vanishing. Meanwhile, other things came tumbling out of the instrument—three balloons, some glittery stars, a pair of socks and . . . a roll of toilet paper.

Hare stopped and looked at the toilet paper with surprise. "I'm so sorry. I have no idea where that came from."

But Wombat was enchanted and she looked at Hare with wonder. "You're a genius!" she told Hare.

"Actually it can be quite annoying," Armadillo interrupted. "Last week I tripped over the puppies and banged my elbow. It was sore for three days. Anyhow, I thought you'd come to mend the light. The fridge is in the kitchen. This way."

Wombat looked at Hare, who put down his tuba and made a sign with his thumb, so Wombat fell in behind Armadillo.

Armadillo held the door open for Wombat and they went through to the kitchen. Armadillo half covered his mouth with one paw and whispered loudly to Hare, "We'd better keep an eye on Wombat. Fridge-light menders don't arrive on bicycles performing tricks. She might be a cat burglar."

"But she's not a cat," laughed Hare. "She's a wombat."

Armadillo gave Hare a stern frown. "You

know what I mean. It's all very suspicious."

But Wombat did mend the fridge light. She took out the old bulb. She got a new one from the basket on her bicycle. She screwed it into place in the fridge and it lit up at once.

"There!" she said.

Armadillo looked at it. After all, it might suddenly go out. A light bulb from a pinging and beeping wombat was not to be trusted. But the bulb didn't go out. It worked just as a proper light bulb should and it lit up everything inside the fridge, especially the splendid new lump of cheese from the store.

Armadillo opened and closed the fridge door several times. Whenever he opened the door, the light came on. Armadillo had to admit Wombat had done a good job.

"Thank you," he said as Wombat left.

"That's okay," beamed Wombat, jumping back on her bike. She beeped and she pinged.

She did a headstand on the seat. Wombat waved back at Armadillo and Hare with all four paws in the air.

The two friends watched her until she went around a corner and vanished from sight.

"Extraordinary," said Hare. "What a creature!"

"Yes," said Armadillo. "But I do think it odd. I mean, why do all that stuff? Why not just arrive, do the job, and go?" He shook his head. "Still," he added, "one must always say 'thank you' for a job well done."

"Maybe Wombat likes doing tricks on her bike," said Hare.

"Yes, yes, I can understand that, Hare. But why mend fridge lights as well? It's so odd. I mean, it's unheard of!"

From the distance came the sound of a far-off *ping-ping*, followed by a *beep-beep*.

Hare gave a faint smile. "Not anymore," he said. He picked up his tuba and began to play once again. Out popped a kitten or three, a rather pretty tea towel, a bouquet of flowers, and—

"Oh, another roll of toilet paper," murmured Hare. He rested the big instrument on the floor, and his ears and head disappeared inside for a moment. "I don't know. Most mysterious. I think my tuba must be feeling out of sorts today. Perhaps it will be better tomorrow."

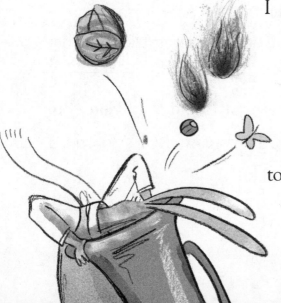

But Hare found he was talking to himself. Armadillo had gone back to his painting.

Hare went and stood beside his friend, cleaned his glasses, and studied the new work.

"I do like this one," said Hare admiringly.

"Thank you, Hare." Armadillo stood back and studied the canvas. "Of course, it's not finished yet."

"I can tell," said Hare. "Because there's a piece missing on the sandwich, just there."

"No, it's not missing," Armadillo corrected. "I ate that piece."

"Oh," said Hare. "Well, I hope it tasted nice."

The Visitor

A jaguar came to the forest clearing. Jaguar was sleek and beautiful. She was also hungry. She knocked on the door of Armadillo and Hare's log cabin.

"Do you have anything to eat?" asked Jaguar hopefully.

Armadillo noted Jaguar's sharp teeth. He wedged the door with one foot, just in case.

"What would you like?" he asked.

"Anything. I'm hungry." Jaguar flopped down. She lay right across Armadillo's front door.

"Do you eat mice?"

Jaguar pulled a face. "Never. They are far too small."

"Elephants?" suggested Armadillo.

"Too big," said Jaguar, shaking her beautiful head.

Armadillo cleared his throat. "*Er-hmm.* Armadillos?"

Jaguar considered this. "I have never seen one. My grandfather told me that he tried to eat an armadillo once, unsuccessfully. That was a long time ago."

Armadillo wedged his other foot against the door. He tried to ask what happened. His voice came out as an awkward squeak and he had to repeat himself. "W-what happened?"

Jaguar sighed deeply. "Apparently the armadillo curled up into a ball."

"Yes! Yes! That's what I would do!" Armadillo said excitedly. He quickly stopped and lowered his voice. "I . . . I mean, that is to say, that's what armadillos do!"

Jaguar looked at Armadillo in an interested kind of way.

"They do curl up into a tight ball," Armadillo quickly agreed.

Jaguar still looked interested.

"So I'm told."

"Hmm." Jaguar considered this for a

moment. "Have you ever seen one?" she asked.

Armadillo didn't like to lie. "Yes, I've seen one," he said, and left it at that.

The two animals gazed at each other. Armadillo managed a nervous smile. Jaguar picked at her teeth with a wisp of grass.

"Hares are quite tasty," she observed.

Armadillo gulped. He was glad Hare was safely upstairs, reading. "I— I—I . . . could make you a cheese sandwich."

"What's a cheese sandwich?" asked Jaguar, frowning. "It's not vegetarian, is it?"

Armadillo thought it was best to avoid

answering the second of Jaguar's questions. "It's two thick slices of bread with cheese between. I could put some pickle on it too. Pickles are nice."

Armadillo wished he didn't sound so nervous. He couldn't help it. He was nervous.

"All right. Make me a cheese sandwich," said Jaguar heavily. "No pickle."

"Good. Wait there a moment. I'll be back in a jiffy."

"What's a 'jiffy'?" asked Jaguar.

"It's a minuscule piece of time," Armadillo explained, but Jaguar still looked confused. Armadillo turned to go to the kitchen.

As he did so, Hare called from upstairs. "Did I hear a visitor at the door? I'll come down."

Jaguar's ears pricked up at once. She lifted her graceful head and sniffed the air. "Have you got someone upstairs?"

"There's no need to come down, Elephant," Armadillo said loudly, so Hare would hear. "It's only Jaguar."

Jaguar was astonished. She craned her neck and gazed up the stairs. "How did you manage to get an elephant up there?"

"Oh, it's extraordinary what movers can do these days. Pianos, giant wardrobes, elephants— it's easy for them." Armadillo smiled brightly. "Let me get you that sandwich."

He hurried off to the kitchen. He made the sandwich as quickly as he could.

"One cheese sandwich, no pickle," said Armadillo, returning to the front door.

Jaguar sat up. She ate the sandwich in one bite. "Chewy," she complained. "And that

yellow meat was definitely very odd."

"Perhaps it's an acquired taste," suggested Armadillo.

"I don't even know what that means," Jaguar told him. She cleaned her teeth with a fresh blade of grass. "'Minuscule'? 'Acquired'? Long words give me a headache."

Armadillo fell silent. Jaguar slowly got to her feet. She stretched and slouched off. Armadillo watched her as she slowly padded all the way back to the forest and then the trees swallowed her up.

"So beautiful," murmured Armadillo, shaking his head. "And so dangerous."

The next day Armadillo and Hare sat on the bench by the front door. They were watching the sunlight filter through the leaves. It made patterns on the meadow beside the forest.

"It's a shame about Jaguar," said Hare. "I would have liked to have met her. We might have been friends."

Armadillo grunted. "I know. It's good to
make friends, but sometimes it's difficult." He
patted Hare's paw. "I was afraid Jaguar would
eat you." Armadillo watched a single leaf slowly
twirl down, down, and around. At last it settled

on the grass in a patch of
sunlight. "We can't be friends
with everybody," he added.

The pair gazed out through
the quiet trees.

"You're right," sighed Hare
after a while. "We can't be friends with everybody. Not when they have such sharp teeth.
You know, Armadillo, you can be very wise
sometimes."

Armadillo gave a quiet chuckle. "Sometimes
is better than none-times. Anyhow, I don't
think Jaguar liked my sandwich. That was a
waste of a good piece of cheese. Still, at least I
didn't put any pickle on it. I do like pickles."

There was a sunlit silence.

A smile drifted across Armadillo's wrinkled

face. "You know, Hare, it might have been all right if Jaguar's teeth had been made of rubber."

"Oh, I like that!" laughed Hare. He leaned back against the bench and let the warm sun play upon his ears.

"What an exquisite creature Jaguar is," murmured Armadillo dreamily. "Such elegant beauty." Then he frowned. "Mind you, she might well be one of the most beautiful creatures in the forest, but she has no manners, Hare. None. That cheese sandwich I made especially for her—she didn't even say 'thank you.' No manners at all!"

But Armadillo's words fell on deaf ears.

Hare had fallen asleep in the sun.

The Storm

The wind had spent all day blowing things every which way. Leaves and bits of twig whirled through the air before being hurled to the ground, scattering around the meadow. Almost all the animals stayed indoors or looked for shelter somewhere.

Hare wanted to go for a run, but the moment he went outside, the wind caught his scarf and whisked it away. He managed to grab hold of it just as the wind tried to toss it high into a tree. Hare hurried back inside and shut the door.

"I thought the wind would blow my head off," he told Armadillo.

"It's certainly blustery," Armadillo answered. He gazed out the window and considered the gloomy sky and heavy clouds. "I think there might be a storm on the way."

"Oh." Hare's face paled.

Armadillo patted his friend on the back. He knew Hare didn't like storms. Thunder was noisy. Lightning was flashy. It was all far too surprising. Storms made Hare jump and did strange things to his long ears.

By the time they went to bed, the wind was even stronger. Hare tried to settle down to sleep in his room, but his window rattled and banged. The gale howled around the corners of the little log cabin and scratched wildly at the roof. On top of that he could hear Armadillo snoring next door. He thought about playing his tuba so he couldn't hear the gale. But then he might wake Armadillo, so he didn't.

The first flash of lightning had Hare sitting straight up in bed. His fur was on end and his ears twisted together in a frantic spiral. A few moments later the first thunderclap sent his ears

spiraling together in the opposite direction. Hare dived beneath his duvet.

Even Armadillo opened his eyes and tutted to himself. "Hare won't like this," he told himself, and he sat up, pushed his feet into his old red slippers, and went to the next-door bedroom.

All that could be seen of Hare was a shivering, quivering hump in the middle of the bed. Armadillo put one quiet paw on the hump.

"Come on," he said to Hare. "We'll share the storm between us. Then it won't be so bad."

So Armadillo made them both some chamomile tea. He took it upstairs and they climbed into Armadillo's big bed. Armadillo was quite heavy. The mattress went almost down to the ground on his side, pushing Hare almost up to the ceiling on his side.

Now they watched the storm, with its frantic display of lightning and sudden noises. Armadillo felt it was always better to actually see what was making so much fuss.

"It's like being at the theater, Hare. I do think it's wonderful. Don't you think it's beautiful?"

No. Hare didn't. He was far too scared to see any beauty in it at all. He jumped every time there was a bang. Even so, he was glad Armadillo was so brave, and when a sudden extra-flashy double lightning bolt sent Hare's ears scrabbling wildly into a knot, it was Armadillo who untied them.

"Did you know," Armadillo began, "that if you count the seconds from the flash to the bang, you can work out how far away the storm is?"

"No. I didn't know that," said Hare, nervously holding on to both his ears, just in case.

"You divide the number of seconds by five, and that's how many miles away it is. Let's wait for a lightning strike and we'll count together."

There was a flash. "One, two, three . . ." began Armadillo. "Eight, nine, ten . . ." *BANG!*

"Ten seconds," Armadillo declared. "That means the storm is two miles away."

Hare was relieved. Two miles seemed quite a long way off for something that made so much noise. They waited until the next flash. Fifteen seconds later, thunder shook the ink-black sky once again.

"Now the storm is three miles away," observed Armadillo. "That means it's going."

"Good," said Hare, and Armadillo noticed that Hare's ears were a little woozy and had collapsed onto his shoulders.

The storm drifted off and both animals fell asleep.

In the morning, it was Hare who woke first. Sunlight was streaming into the room. What a difference! His heart lifted and so did his ears. Hare decided it was just the morning for a run. He left Armadillo sleeping and went to his own room to change. The first thing he did was pull back the curtains.

Oh! A big face was staring at him through the glass. It was Elephant. Hare opened the window. "Hello! What are you doing here, Elephant?"

"Oh my! I've had such a night! Phoowee!

The wind howled. Bang-crash! Trees falling down. Branches whipping around. Leaves all over the place. Sheesh! I thought I had better go to an open space where nothing could fall on me. So I came to the meadow. Then, when the sun came up, I saw this lovely log cabin. I said to myself, 'Who lives here?' I was just taking a peek when you peeked back, Hare. Is this your bedroom? *Phoowee!* It's fantastical!"

Hare was rather proud of his room. He asked Elephant if he'd like to look inside. Elephant thought that would be splendid. He just managed to push his big head through the open window. He waved his trunk around with enormous excitement.

"*Phoowee!* It's beautiful, Hare. You've got a bed and a chair and a chest of drawers and a wardrobe and a mirror and a carpet and a painting of—pinch my eyes!—a cheese

sandwich. And some flowers and a dressing gown and a—"

"Yes, everything I need," interrupted Hare. He was afraid Elephant would never stop. "Armadillo painted the picture," he said. "He mostly paints cheese sandwiches."

"It's lovely," said Elephant. "Strange, but lovely. Is Armadillo's room the same?"

"His is bigger," Hare told him.

"Even bigger? Oh my! I must see that," said Elephant. He pulled his head back. At least, he tried—but he couldn't because his big ears were jammed against the window frame. There was no way he could extract himself.

"Maybe if I give a really big tug . . ." suggested Elephant, and he did. There was an enormous crack and a creak and a squeak, and at last Elephant's head popped out. Unfortunately so did the window frame. In fact the frame was now firmly stuck around Elephant's neck.

"Oh my!" murmured Elephant.

Armadillo had been woken by the dreadful noise and he hurried into Hare's room.

"I thought I heard a—Oh! Elephant! Hmm. You seem to have Hare's window stuck around your neck."

"Yes," said Elephant, a trifle embarrassed. "I noticed that too. Sorry."

Hare looked anxiously at Armadillo. He wondered if Armadillo would be cross.

Armadillo folded his front paws across his chest. "Well, I have to say you've saved us a lot of bother, Elephant. I have wanted to change that window and get a new one for quite a while. It rattles in the wind. It leaks and lets the rain in. It was doing exactly that in the storm we've just had. Now Hare can have a new window."

"What about the old one?" asked Elephant.

He carefully touched the dangling window frame with his trunk.

"Oh, you can keep that," said Armadillo dismissively.

"But how will I get it off?" Elephant asked.

Hare looked at Armadillo and was sure there was a twinkle in his friend's eyes.

Armadillo shrugged. "I have no idea, Elephant. You put it on, so you can take it off. Perhaps it will remind you not to stick your big head into small spaces."

"*Phoowee,*" murmured Elephant. He turned away and wandered back into the forest.

As the big beast disappeared from sight, Hare turned to Armadillo.

"I don't think Elephant has any idea of just how big he really is."

"I know what you mean," said Armadillo, and he began to chuckle. "It's extraordinary really. Ha ha! Elephant has caused far more damage than the thunderstorm!"

Armadillo chuckled again, and soon the two friends had to cling to each other as they doubled over with laughter.

Nobody's Birthday Party

It was nobody's birthday, which was disappointing. Usually if there was a birthday to celebrate, there would be a party. Tortoise liked parties. His life was rather predictable and slow—his slowness being what was also predictable. No parties meant no excitement, so Tortoise had called a meeting to discuss the problem, and most of the forest animals were there.

"It's nobody's birthday," Tortoise told everyone. "But we could still have a party. It can be a party for nobody."

Tortoise's announcement was greeted with

cheers and laughter, but Lobster could see a problem.

"You can't have a party for nobody," she declared. "Nobody will come."

"*Au contraire*," said Tortoise (who had a French mother, Madame Tortue). "Everybody will come because everybody will be invited."

Lobster folded her claws with a faint  clack. "If everybody comes, it won't be for nobody," she pointed out crisply.

Armadillo nudged Hare. "I used to like Lobster," he

murmured. "But I'm not sure now."

"No, no. I think Lobster has a point." Hare smoothed back his ears and let them ping straight back up.

"Maybe she has, but her point misses the point." Armadillo shook his head. "If you understand me." He wasn't sure if he understood himself. He scratched his long nose with both front paws. It always seemed to go wrinkly when he was confused. "The other point being that it is nobody's birthday."

Hare considered this. "I thought that was the point."

Armadillo took a deep breath and sighed. Then he asked loudly, "Is there going to be a party or not?"

The forest animals decided there would be

a party. Not only that, but there would be food and dancing.

When they got home Hare noticed a change in Armadillo. He couldn't stop muttering to himself and he was unable to settle down anywhere.

"Dancing! *Hrrrrmph!* Dancing! *Pfffff!*"

Hare couldn't stand it any longer. "Whatever is the matter?"

Armadillo shook his head. He gazed at his feet as if they had committed a terrible crime. "It's the dancing," he said at last. "I'm simply not very good at it. It's all right for you, Hare. You're a frisky fellow, but I'm not the right shape. There, I've said it. Now you know, and I feel stupid."

Hare smiled and took Armadillo by the

shoulders. "Don't worry. Dancing is easier than you think. I'll teach you."

He put some music on.

"Just do what I do," said Hare cheerfully. He was a good dancer. He moved in time to the music, which is a good thing if you're dancing.

Armadillo tried to follow. He bumped into an armchair. He fell across it and rolled onto the floor.

"Interesting move," said Hare cheerfully. "Let's try again."

They tried again and again. Somehow Armadillo hit the furniture every time. Hare moved all the furniture out of the room.

Armadillo lurched into Hare instead. They both fell over. Hare got to his feet. He straightened up his crumpled ears. His cheerfulness was badly bruised. So were his elbows, shoulder, and tail.

"You know," said Hare, helping his friend to his feet, "you are wise and kind and lots of good things. But you really can't dance."

Armadillo grunted. "I had better stay at home then while you go to the party."

"Stop being so grumpy. We shall go to the party together," said Hare. "We shall sit down. You can eat cheese sandwiches and we shall watch the dancing."

So Armadillo and Hare got ready for Nobody's birthday party. Hare looked dashing in his best scarf and had decided to take his tuba. Armadillo wore sunglasses and a black leather jacket. He had wanted to wear his cardigan.

"I am not going to anyone's birthday party with you in your cardigan," Hare had said firmly.

"I am not going to Anyone's birthday party," argued Armadillo. "It's Nobody's birthday party."

"Ha ha," said Hare rather crossly. But chuckles bubbled up inside him. Soon they had to hold each other up in case the laughter knocked them right over.

They arrived at the party in a very good mood. This was made even better when they found the beach and edge of the forest festooned with little colored lights, which turned out to be the fireflies and glowworms from all around.

The band started up and everyone sang "Happy Birthday" to Nobody. Lots of animals danced. But Hare kept his promise. He sat down with Armadillo and they watched the dancing.

Armadillo could see Hare's feet twitching in time to the music. He was about to tell Hare to join in, when Lobster approached them both.

"I didn't think you'd come, Lobster," muttered Armadillo.

"Oh, I can't miss any dancing. I love to dance. So, Armadillo, will you, won't you, will you, won't you dance with me?"

Armadillo was instantly alarmed. But Armadillo was also polite and he didn't know how to refuse. He began to get to his feet, but Hare pulled him back.

"I'm sorry, Lobster. Armadillo isn't

allowed to dance. Doctor's orders. He has a very bad knee. In fact," Hare added, "he has four bad knees. One on each leg."

Lobster looked disappointed.

"I'm sorry," said Armadillo, secretly relieved. "Maybe I could dance with you?" Hare smiled at Lobster. But Lobster's face suddenly lit up. She was staring over

Hare's shoulder with delight. "Oh!" she gasped. "There's Giraffe! I must dance with him! He has such wonderfully long, elegant legs. Don't you think?"

Armadillo turned and squinted. "Lovely legs," he agreed. "But there are too many of them."

Lobster was puzzled. "He only has four legs."

Armadillo seemed surprised. "Four? It always looks to me as if he's got at least fifteen."

Lobster's alarmed eyes glanced at Hare for reassurance.

"Armadillo is joking," Hare explained.

"Oh! Ha ha. Of course." Lobster hurried off to dance with Giraffe. She didn't speak to Armadillo or Hare for the rest of the evening.

Armadillo turned to his friend. "Thank you

for saving me from making a fool of myself on the dance floor."

Hare smiled. "Oh, I didn't just save you, old friend. I saved everyone. You would have caused chaos!" But Hare's long legs couldn't stop twitching. "I'm sorry, I just can't keep still any longer. I must do something. I think I shall join the band for a number or two."

"Yes," nodded Armadillo. "Do go and play."

So Hare joined the band and he played so beautifully that his tuba soon filled the air with cupcakes and lollipops, floating lanterns that rose high in the night sky, rainbows and glitter that rained gently down upon the dancers. When he finished, all the animals clapped. Hare took a bow and his ears made a deep bow of their own.

Hare went back to sit with Armadillo, who patted him on the back.

"That was magical," Armadillo said somewhat sadly. "Listen, Hare. Do you think that if I had proper lessons, I would end up being able to dance? I mean, if I really tried?"

Hare counted his bruises. His elbows still hurt and his tail felt rather sensitive. "We can overcome so much by trying and trying again," he agreed.

Armadillo leaned forward eagerly. "Exactly. That's what I was thinking."

"But sometimes we just have to accept our limitations," Hare went on. "Sometimes there

are things we shall never be able to do, and never should."

"I see," murmured Armadillo. He sank back into his chair. "So that's a 'no,' is it?"

"Yes," nodded Hare. "It's a 'no.'"

When Armadillo and Hare eventually headed home, Nobody's birthday party was still going strong. They reached the meadow. The moon and stars were shining down on it so brightly they could even see all the flowers of the meadow laid out before them, like tiny stars that had fallen from the sky and landed at their feet. The two friends stopped in amazement.

Hare sat on a tree stump and took up his tuba. "I have never seen such a beautiful dance floor. Armadillo, it's all yours."

The most wonderful slow waltz drifted out of Hare's tuba and weaved and wafted its melodious way across the meadow. Armadillo couldn't help but follow it, dancing, whirling, twirling, falling over, laughing, and swirling some more. His only partners were the dozens of bats that flittered and jittered around his head as he danced all the way to the cabin, and there the music stopped.

Hare crossed the meadow and joined Armadillo on the front steps. Hare beamed at his friend. "Now that was magical," he said, and they went indoors.

Giants

One afternoon Hare and Armadillo decided to walk down to the sea's edge. It was a fine day—the sort of day one wanted to be outside.

"I might go paddling," said Armadillo bravely.

"We can take a picnic," suggested Hare. "Some afternoon tea."

Armadillo nodded. "Good idea, Hare. I shall get it ready."

A little later they set off from their cabin. The path to the sea went around the edge of the forest. Sometimes Armadillo might say

something. Sometimes Hare would say something. But mostly they walked in silence and listened to the wind and the birds. They took turns carrying the picnic. They had almost reached the little beach when someone called out to them.

"Hello," said whoever-it-was-who-said-it.

"Hello," Hare answered. They both looked around but could see nothing.

"I'm over here," said the voice.

Armadillo and Hare turned toward the sound. All they could see were bushes and a tree here and there.

"Here," repeated the voice. "I'm waving at you."

"Oh," said Hare. He glanced at Armadillo.

Armadillo's eyebrows went up. He shook his head.

"Can you wave again?" Armadillo called out. "We still can't see you."

"I'm here, right in front of you," said the voice. "Look, I'm waving two legs now."

Armadillo and Hare hunted and hunted. They still saw nothing.

"It's me, Stick Insect," said the voice. "I'm on the bush right in front of you, near the top. You see the white flower? It's on the end of the twig I'm standing on. I'm going to wave four legs now. Wait a moment. It's a bit difficult. I've only got two legs left to hang on with. Okay, here goes.

There! Can you see me now?"

Hare and Armadillo peered at the bush as close as they could. They didn't want to get a poke in the eye from the bush's branches. It didn't matter though, because they still couldn't see Stick Insect.

Hare didn't want to hurt Stick Insect's feelings, so he pretended. "Oh, there you are!" he said. He nudged Armadillo.

Armadillo gave a grunt. "Oh! Oh, yes. There you are, Stick Insect. How are you?"

"I'm fine, thank you. Isn't it a lovely day?"

"Yes, it is. We're going for a picnic on the beach," Hare explained. "Armadillo is going paddling. You can come too, if you like."

Armadillo grunted again. "Have we got enough food?" he whispered to Hare.

"I don't think Stick Insect eats that much," Hare whispered back.

"I'd like to come," said Stick Insect, "but I'm having my hair done this afternoon."

"Oh," said Hare, somewhat surprised. "Maybe we shall see you later then."

"That would be nice," said Stick Insect. "Bye-bye."

Armadillo and Hare carried on down to the beach. They spread a little rug on the sand. They put out their picnic and sat down. Armadillo was laughing to himself.

"I was just thinking, Hare. I hope we do see Stick Insect later, because we never saw her the first time. She's invisible!"

"Do you think she really is invisible?" asked Hare.

"It could be that we simply couldn't see her," Armadillo replied.

"Isn't that the same thing?"

"No, not necessarily." Armadillo studied Hare. "Sometimes I can't see your whiskers, but I know they are there."

"Of course my whiskers are there," said Hare. He gave them a quick tweak. "Oh, look,

Lobster is coming to see us."

"Don't ask her if she'd like to join us," Armadillo said quickly in a low voice. "I only made a picnic for two, and you've already tried to give half of it to Stick Insect."

But Lobster didn't want anything to eat. She was far too excited.

"I had such an amazing dream last night,"

she told Armadillo and Hare. "Actually it was more of a vision than a dream."

"Really?" muttered Armadillo. "A vision?"

"Yes, yes! It was as if I were flying in the sky. I went up so high, far above the clouds. You will never guess what I saw. Do you know what is beyond the clouds?"

Hare and Armadillo shook their heads. Lobster leaned forward, her eyes shining bright.

"The Giant Lobster in the Sky!" she announced.

"A giant lobster?" repeated Armadillo.

"No, no, not *a* giant lobster," cried Lobster. "The Giant Lobster in the Sky. And she spoke to me. She told me that I would always be safe and she would always look after me."

"That's nice," said Hare. "What else happened in your dream?"

"I thanked the Giant Lobster in the Sky and I flew home. Then I woke up. I'm so excited. It was a vision! There is a Giant Lobster in the Sky!" Lobster clacked her claws like castanets. "I must go and tell everyone. Isn't it amazing!" She hurried up the beach.

Armadillo picked up a cheese sandwich. He munched on it for a while. Hare chewed on a lettuce- and-carrot quiche.

"I had a dream like Lobster's," said Armadillo after a while. "It was a long time ago, but I remember it well. The thing is, I was flying too, but I didn't see a Giant Lobster.

I saw a Giant Armadillo."

"Really?" said Hare. "Did the Giant Armadillo speak to you?"

Armadillo slowly shook his head. "No. He was too busy brushing his teeth."

Hare's ears gave a surprised twitch, but he didn't say anything. They watched the little waves break almost at their feet, over and over again.

"The thing is," Armadillo said, poking the sand thoughtfully with a stick, "I saw a Giant Armadillo and Lobster saw a Giant Lobster, so maybe there might be a Giant Hare up there too." Armadillo nodded at Hare. "Or a Giant Wombat," he added. His face suddenly brightened. "Or what about a Giant Invisible Stick Insect?"

"Now you're just being silly," said Hare.

They fell silent. They gazed out across the sea and watched the sun set. It flooded the sky with red and gold. The waves became red and gold too, shimmering as they danced across the sand.

"Beautiful," sighed Hare.

"Yes." Armadillo nodded.

"Heavenly," murmured something invisible.

A Flood and an
Interesting Cardigan

The rain had been falling from a flat gray sky for days. Everyone had been stuck indoors. Boredom was their only visitor. Armadillo had painted eight pictures of cheese sandwiches. Hare had read fifteen books. He wasn't supposed to play his tuba indoors, but he did. What else could he do? He played it quietly. It was a rainy-day tune. Frogs gently plopped out of the instrument. They hopped around for a while until they became fainter and fainter and finally vanished.

"I know you're bored," sighed Armadillo. "But I think we have enough wet-weather problems without you filling the house with frogs."

"They've gone now," Hare pointed out. "Anyhow, you've been filling the house with cheese sandwiches. Eight of them. Eight!"

"There's nothing wrong with cheese sandwiches," Armadillo grumbled.

"That is a matter of opinion," snapped Hare. He suddenly felt so annoyed he blew hard and noisily into his tuba. There was an explosive note and out flew an old boot. Armadillo had to duck as it cartwheeled past his ear. It hit the eighth painting. Both boot and picture fell to the floor. The boot slowly disappeared, like the frogs. But it left behind a large, muddy footprint right across the sandwich in the painting.

Hare and Armadillo looked at the ruined

painting. Armadillo was silent. Hare shifted uneasily in his chair.

"Sorry," he said.

"It's the rain," Armadillo grunted. "It's getting on our nerves. Anyhow, you're right. Eight cheese sandwiches is far too many. I should have stopped at seven."

Hare looked out of the window. He could see nothing but water. "I think we're marooned," he told Armadillo. "The lake has overflowed.

We're surrounded by water."

Armadillo wrinkled his long nose. He was thinking. "If the rain doesn't stop soon, the water will rise even higher. Some of the forest animals will have problems. Wombat, for example, and Tortoise."

"What about us?" asked Hare. "Suppose the water floods the house?"

"That could happen," agreed Armadillo. "I don't suppose you can play a tune on your tuba that makes large sponges fly out of it? Sponges might be useful for mopping things up."

Hare shook his head. They both looked again at the painting with the footprint. "I never know what will come out of my tuba."

"Evidently," muttered Armadillo.

The log cabin began to creak and groan. It

shook. It shifted around as if a small earthquake had grabbed ahold of it. It wasn't an earthquake. It was the flood. The water rose up around and under the log cabin. Their little home was now floating on the surface.

The two friends stared out at nothing but water. They stumbled slightly as little waves caught the house and turned it slowly, around and around.

"What shall we do?" asked Hare.

"I don't know," Armadillo answered.

Hare's ears collapsed. "That's not much use."

"I know it isn't," mumbled Armadillo. "It's a funny thing, but in times of danger I can only think of cheese sandwiches. I find them comforting." Armadillo watched a large log float by. Tortoise was on board. He waved and gave them a weak smile. Armadillo waved

back. He turned to Hare. "Can't you think of anything?"

Hare's ears suddenly sprang upright. "As a matter of fact, I can. Seeing Tortoise has given me an idea."

Hare went to the back of the house. At the rear there was a big porch. Armadillo and Hare kept all kinds of things there. To tell the truth it was more of a dumping place than a porch. There were logs for the fire in winter. There were folded sun loungers for the summer. There were gardening tools for the spring. And there was a canoe with two paddles. That was for any time of year.

Hare grabbed the paddles and hurried back to Armadillo. "Here," he said. "You paddle on this side of the house. I shall go and paddle on the other. We can row our cabin wherever we want to go."

So they did. They opened a window on each side of the house. Armadillo leaned out of one and Hare leaned out of the other. They began paddling.

They hadn't floated very far when Elephant came swimming up to them. He was still wearing his window-necklace.

"Oh my!" cried Elephant. "So much rain! *Phoowee!* I'm having to swim everywhere. You two seem to be all right. Wombat is up a tree, but she keeps falling off. I don't think she's very good at climbing. I can swim underwater, look!" Elephant disappeared beneath the surface. Only the tip of his trunk could be seen as he went on his way.

Hare and Armadillo paddled across to the trees. Wombat was indeed in danger. She was hanging upside down from a branch and about to fall in. Hare and Armadillo steered the cabin until they were close by. Wombat dropped straight down the chimney and landed in the front room along with a cloud of soot.

"That was fun! You saved me. I had to leave my bicycle up a tree. I saw Jaguar earlier, just over there. She could do with some help too."

Armadillo and Hare looked at each other. They didn't want Jaguar in the house. Not with those sharp teeth of hers.

"I've had another idea," said Hare.

"Oh, you're full of ideas today, aren't you?" grunted Armadillo.

"It's more useful than being full of cheese sandwiches," Hare shot back. He returned to the porch. This time he was dragging the canoe. They paddled the cabin across to Jaguar and pushed the canoe beneath her tree.

Jaguar was very happy to climb into it. "But I don't have anything to paddle with," she drawled. "You two have paddles."

"Use your paws," Armadillo said rather sharply.

And that is how things stayed for the next few days. It carried on raining. The waters rose higher. The cabin floated around taking on more animals. Invisible Stick Insect and Wombat were there, and Tortoise. Giraffe stood inside with his neck going up the stairs and his head sticking out of Hare's bedroom window. Soon there was no room and all the food had gone. Every now and then Jaguar would drift past in her canoe.

"Anything to eat?" she would ask, eyeing Armadillo and Hare's motley crew.

The whole log cabin would shout back, "NO!"

But in truth, everyone was hungry.

"I don't suppose you could play your tuba and rustle up some cheese sandwiches?" asked Armadillo. Hare did try, but all that came out were a couple of empty saucepans and a lady's swimsuit.

At last the rain stopped. The sun came out. The water went down. There was a bump and the log cabin settled back almost exactly where it had been before the flood.

Armadillo opened the door and one by one the other animals left.

"Thank you," said Wombat.

"Thank you," said an invisible voice.

"That's all right, Stick Insect. Glad you could join us," said Hare.

"Be careful," warned Armadillo, as a large

brown-and-yellow backside shuffled awkwardly toward them. "I think Giraffe can only come out backward."

With a lot of effort and only one broken stair rod, Giraffe eased himself out of the house. He dipped his head toward Armadillo and Hare. "You saved us all," he said gratefully.

"It was nothing," Hare answered.

"Actually, it was quite a lot," muttered Armadillo. "Especially food-wise. I haven't seen any cheese for two days."

But Giraffe and all the others had departed for their own homes.

Later that evening Hare was brushing his teeth and getting ready for bed. Armadillo came up and stood by the bathroom door.

"You know how you couldn't make cheese sandwiches come out of your tuba?" Armadillo reminded Hare.

"Yes?"

"I've been thinking. If you did make cheese sandwiches in your tuba, would we be able to eat them? I mean, things that come out of your tuba vanish very quickly, don't they?"

116

"Yes?" repeated Hare. He wondered where this questioning was going.

"So if we ate them, would they actually be there?"

"No," said Hare. "They'd be in your stomach."

"You're not understanding me," said Armadillo crossly. "If you eat something that can vanish, have you actually eaten it, or has it vanished? Is it real? It looks real when it comes out, but then it vanishes. So can you eat it?"

Hare thought about this. He remembered the ruined painting. The boot had disappeared. But the footprint it left behind hadn't. What did that mean?

"That's a very good question," Hare told Armadillo at last.

Armadillo sighed deeply. "You don't know

the answer, do you?"

"No," said Hare. "I don't. Neither do you. Maybe some things don't have answers. You may as well ask yourself why you can never put the buttons on your cardigan in the right buttonholes. That's another mystery." Hare smiled. "I'm going to bed. Good night."

Armadillo heaved his shoulders and went to his room. Hare was right. He looked down at his lopsided cardigan. There wasn't an answer to everything.

"And that's what makes it all so interesting," Armadillo told himself.

The Importance of Conversation

Armadillo and Hare were having breakfast. Armadillo had opened a new jar of chutney and was chewing thoughtfully on some cheese.

Hare watched his friend. "Well?"

"Can't talk with my mouth full," Armadillo mumbled.

"You already are," Hare pointed out.

"So are you," Armadillo shot back.

"But I didn't say I couldn't. You're the one who said you couldn't talk with your mouth full, and then you did."

Armadillo ignored him. "I thought I might

take the wheelbarrow to the forest and fetch some wood for winter," he said, changing the subject. "What are you going to do?"

"I shall probably sit in a comfy chair and read," Hare answered. "I like reading."

Armadillo pushed his plate to one side. "What's the book about?"

"Animals. Animals like us. In fact there's a grumpy armadillo in this story who is rather like you."

"Grumpy!" Armadillo pushed his chair back noisily. "I'm not grumpy!"

Hare's whiskers twitched thoughtfully. "Well, let's say 'tetchy' then."

"Tetchy is the same as grumpy; it's just spelled differently," said Armadillo grumpily. Or possibly tetchily.

Hare smiled. "Anyhow, I'm enjoying the book. Don't be too long. I think it's going to rain."

Armadillo went to the door and looked out. The sky was quite clear. "It doesn't look like rain."

Hare shrugged. "I can smell it coming. It will rain sooner or later."

"It's not going to rain sooner," Armadillo declared. "And by the time it's later I shall be back with the logs."

Armadillo fetched the wheelbarrow and set off across the meadow. By the time he reached the edge of the forest, the sky had clouded over and a few spots of rain had pinged off his back. Armadillo grunted and began picking up wood for the fire.

As he searched around for more logs Armadillo noticed that the rain wasn't just battering noisily on his back—it was bouncing off the ground. In fact it wasn't rain. It was hail. Large icy hailstones were clattering through the leaves and smashing into the earth.

Armadillo searched for some kind of shelter and spotted a small cave. He trundled the wheelbarrow into the entrance and settled down to wait until the hail had passed.

The inside of the cave seemed heavy with a kind of sadness. A loud sigh drifted out from the back of the cave and Armadillo peered into the gloom. At first he could see nothing, and then a large hunched and huddled shape became apparent.

A shudder ran down Armadillo's spine. It

was Jaguar, and even as Armadillo watched her carefully, she let out another long sigh. The feeling of sadness was coming from Armadillo's cave companion.

"What's the matter?" he asked.

Jaguar lifted her head slowly. Her eyes glittered in the darkness for a moment as she considered him. "I'm lonely," she said.

Armadillo was rather surprised, but it made him think, and what he thought about was loneliness. He thought about Hare and all the other animals he chatted with: Tortoise, Elephant, Wombat, Invisible Stick Insect, even Lobster. But Jaguar wasn't on the list. Nobody sat down with Jaguar to chat as far as Armadillo knew. Armadillo chewed over this new awareness and decided it was time to speak plainly.

"Well," he began slowly. "The thing is, Jaguar . . . it's the teeth."

"The teeth?" repeated Jaguar, somewhat confused.

"Whose teeth?"

"Yours."

"Mine? My teeth?"

Jaguar was very surprised.

Armadillo nodded. "You do have very sharp teeth. They make you look hungry and it puts off the smaller animals."

"Is that so? Then I have a problem, don't I? I can't take my teeth out. I need them to eat things."

Armadillo nodded. "Exactly. That's what bothers the smaller animals."

Jaguar considered this. Her head slowly sank back to the floor. "Then I suppose I shall be lonely forever."

Armadillo was rather flustered to find himself feeling sorry for Jaguar. He even considered being Jaguar's friend himself, but suppose Jaguar came to the cabin and saw Hare? Hare would be so scared his ears would probably fly right off.

The hailstorm had passed. "I'll think about it," Armadillo told Jaguar. "I'm going home now."

Halfway home Armadillo met Hare, who was carrying two umbrellas. One was over his head and the other was rolled up under his arm.

"I was sure you'd get battered by all that

hail," said Hare a little anxiously. "I brought
you an umbrella."

"Most kind," said Armadillo, but he couldn't

stop thinking about Jaguar. Nobody would be offering her an umbrella.

They walked back to the cabin together. Hare liked kicking the hailstones. Armadillo didn't.

"I'm sorry if I'm grumpy," he told his friend. "Or tetchy," he added, for good measure.

"Oh, it doesn't bother me," Hare said cheerfully. "It's just the way you are."

"*Hmmph.*" Armadillo felt that Hare should be bothered, at least a little bit. Anyhow, Hare was right. It's just the way they were, and Jaguar was just the way she was too.

The friends stacked the logs behind the cabin. Hare studied the neat pile.

"That should last all winter," he declared.

"Don't burn me!" an invisible but familiar

voice piped up.

"Stick Insect? Is that you?" asked Hare.

"Yes. I'm over here, waving. Look— this side. I'm waving like mad. It's good to see you. I haven't spoken to anyone for weeks. At least, when I have, they haven't heard me. I'm small and I look like the sticks I sit on so much that nobody notices. Even worse, I hardly ever see any other stick insects because they look like sticks too. I think I must have said 'good morning' to nothing but twigs at least a thousand times. My camouflage creates a whole different set of problems for a stick insect. Do you see?"

Armadillo shook his head sadly. "Well, no, I

don't exactly see, but then that's your problem, Invisible Stick Insect—not being seen. It's just the way you are. However, I do understand what you are saying and, do you know, I think I have the answer. Now then, if I pick up this log, can you tell me if you are on it?"

"No! This one. I'm waving at you again."

Armadillo looked at Hare and raised his eyebrows in despair. "This one?" he asked, full of hope.

"You found me!" cried Invisible Stick Insect.

Armadillo muttered a silent prayer of thanks. "Good. Now then, hang on tight, Invisible Stick Insect. We're going on a little journey."

"Shall I come?" asked Hare.

"Oh no, no, that wouldn't be a good idea at

all," said Armadillo. "You wait here, Hare, and I shall tell you all about it when I return. I'm going back to the forest."

*

And that is exactly what Armadillo did. He went into the forest carrying the log, and Invisible Stick Insect chatted with Armadillo the whole way there. In fact she talked so much Armadillo was worn out with listening. But then he told himself that the poor little insect had not been able to have a conversation for such a long time.

At length they reached the cave and went inside. Armadillo called out to see if Jaguar was still there.

"Yes, I am," Jaguar drawled. "Why do you ask? Is it lunch time?"

"No, it isn't," answered Armadillo.

"Oh, goodness!" cried Invisible Stick Insect. "Jaguar wants to eat me!"

"Of course she doesn't," said Armadillo. "Jaguar only likes to eat the small animals."

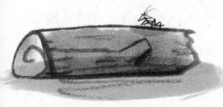

"But I am small!" protested Invisible Stick Insect.

Armadillo chuckled quietly. "You are a lot more than small. You are positively microscopic."

"Oh," said Invisible Stick Insect. "I like that word."

Jaguar growled quietly. "Armadillo likes long words," she said. "Now show me who you are talking to, Armadillo. I can't see a thing."

Armadillo put down the log. Jaguar padded over and sniffed at it. She stared hard. "I can't see anything," she complained.

"Oh, for heaven's sake!" shouted Invisible Stick Insect. "Why is everyone so blind? I'm right here, under your nose!"

Jaguar stepped back sharply. "Oh, yes! Ha ha! Goodness me, you are small, aren't you, and so well camouflaged. Of course, I'm rather well camouflaged myself with my spots, but you are so much like a stick it's almost impossible to see you."

"I know," laughed Invisible Stick Insect. "Do you know, there was one time when . . ."

And that was how Invisible Stick Insect and Jaguar became best friends.

*

Armadillo went back to the log cabin. Hare made tea and got out some very nice cake—a cheesecake, Armadillo's favorite.

As he sat down in his armchair with his tea and cake, Armadillo smiled. "I'm so glad Invisible Stick Insect and Jaguar have become friends. Stick Insect is such a chatterbox. It's nice to think that she is now happily chewing Jaguar's ear off."

Armadillo paused and then chuckled loudly.

"Not literally, of course," he added. "Now then, let's have some cheesecake."

Armadillo and Hare's Short Discussion

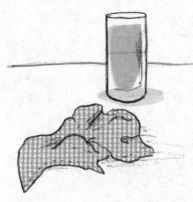

Armadillo had done all the dishes. Now he was doing the drying too. Hare was sitting cross-legged in an old armchair. He was wearing a blue scarf and he was reading. As he read he would tug at one ear, let it spring back up, and then tug it again, over and over. It was just something he did when he was concentrating. Armadillo carefully dried two glasses with the tea towel. He cleared his throat rather noisily.

"Hare?"

"Yes?"

"Tell me, what is it you do?"

"What do you mean, what do I do?"

"Well, I've been wondering," said Armadillo. He examined the glass he had just finished drying. "What do you do?"

Hare's ears flicked moodily. "I don't do anything," he said. "I just am."

"Oh." Armadillo put the glasses away and began drying the plates.

Hare lifted his book. He began to read again, but then he put down his book. He laid it flat on his lap. Hare gazed into the distance for a while. He opened his mouth to say something, then stopped. He stared a bit more, took off his glasses, and at last he spoke.

"So tell me, Armadillo, what do you do?"

The two friends studied each other. Armadillo considered the question. He looked

at it this way and he looked at it that way. Eventually he came to a conclusion.

"Good question," Armadillo said. "I suppose I just am too." Then he smiled and threw the tea towel across the room. It fell over Hare's head. "But you can finish drying the dishes."

Armadillo's Best Cheese Sandwich

Two slices of bread

NOTE 1: Must be same size so cheese doesn't fall out.

Cheese

NOTE 2: Obviously. Cheddar is the best.

Method:

Place cheese between slices of bread.
NOTE 3: *No butter required. Mustn't spoil the full flavor of the cheese.*

Eat: Place in mouth between teeth.
Grip tightly. Pull off large chunk. Chew.

Swallow.
NOTE 4: *Close eyes and emit sighs of intense pleasure.*
NOTE 5: *Offer similar sandwich to Hare but not so big. He has small teeth.*
NOTE 6: *Chutney can be added but sparingly. See above about not spoiling the full flavor.*

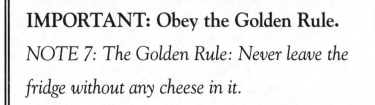

IMPORTANT: Obey the Golden Rule.
NOTE 7: *The Golden Rule: Never leave the fridge without any cheese in it.*